Atlantic

G. Brian Karas

G. P. Putnam's Sons   New York

G. P. PUTNAM'S SONS,

a division of Penguin Putnam Books for Young Readers,
345 Hudson Street, New York, NY 10014.
G. P. Putnam's Sons, Reg. U.S. Pat. & Tm. Off.
Published simultaneously in Canada.
Printed in Hong Kong by South China Printing Co. (1988) Ltd.
Book designed by Gina DiMassi.
Text set in Hoosker.
The art was prepared in gouache, acrylic and pencil.
Library of Congress Cataloging-in-Publication Data
Karas, G. Brian. Atlantic / G. Brian Karas. p. cm.
Summary: Explore what the Atlantic Ocean is, how far it stretches,
how the moon affects it, and other characteristics as
described by the ocean itself. [1. Atlantic Ocean—Fiction.
2. Ocean—Fiction.] I. Title. PZ7.K1296 At 2002 [E]—dc21 2001019602
ISBN 0-399-23632-5
1 3 5 7 9 10 8 6 4 2
First Impression

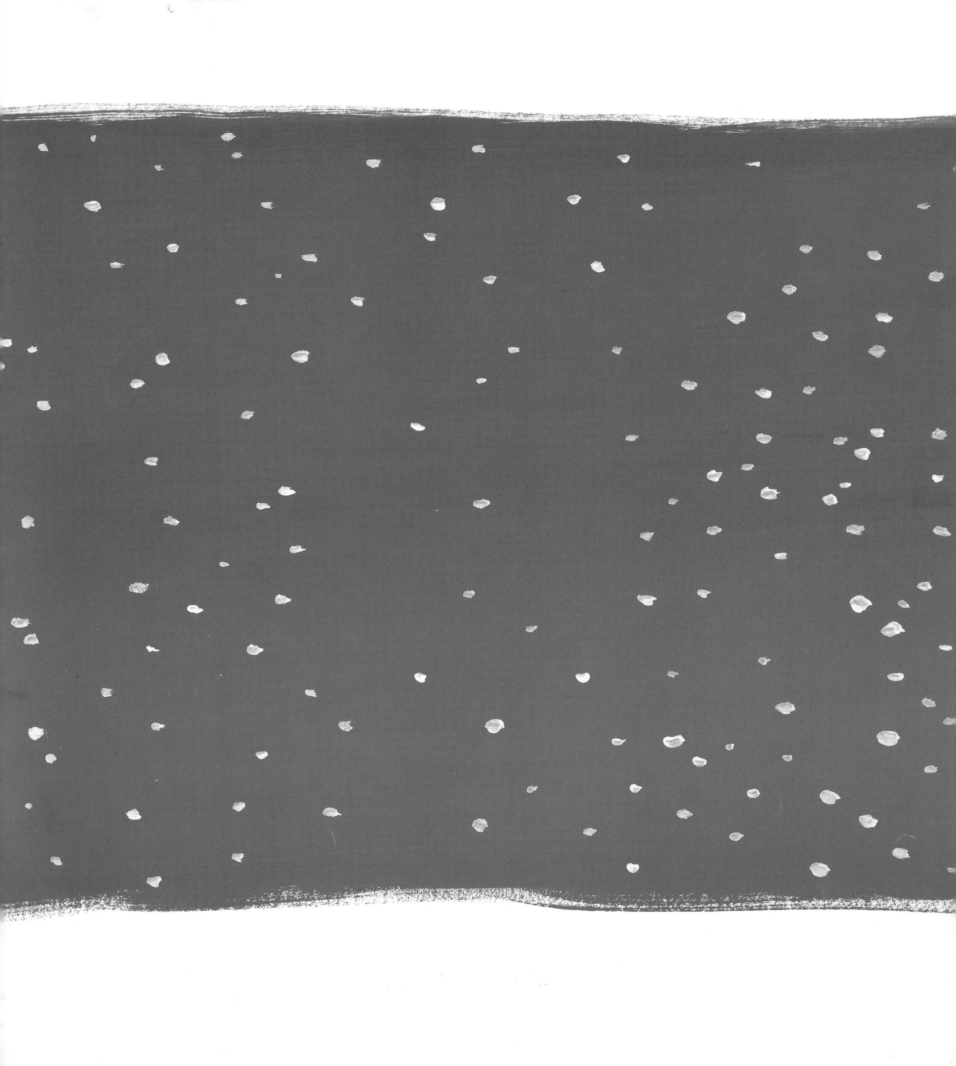

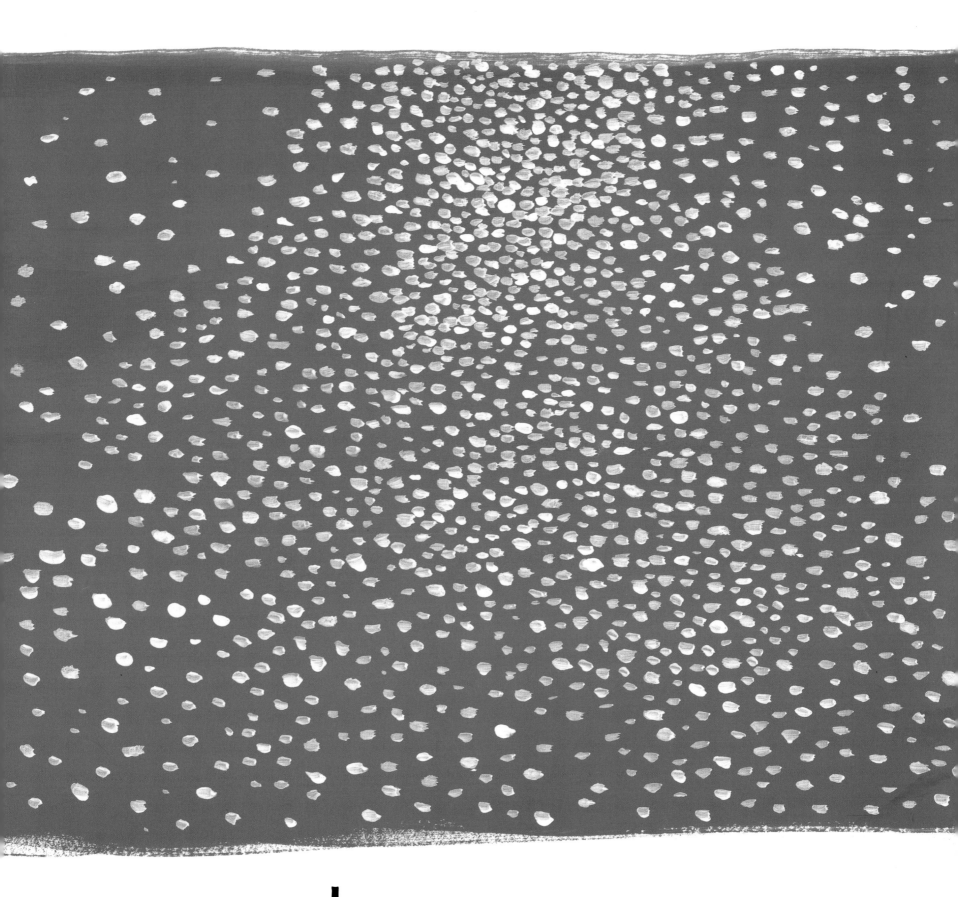

I am the Atlantic Ocean

I begin where the land runs out
at the end of yards
and streets
and hills

I am the blue water at the beach,
the waves,
mist and storms
That salty smell is me too

I stretch from the icy poles,
   North and South
I rub shoulders with North America
   and bump into Africa
I slosh around South America and crash into Europe

But I don't end there
The Pacific and Indian,
Arctic and Antarctic
are my relatives
We are one big family

My water doesn't stay in just one place It travels from continent to continent

So that iceberg floating past someone's window one day

will sometime find itself lapping at your toes on a warm, sandy beach

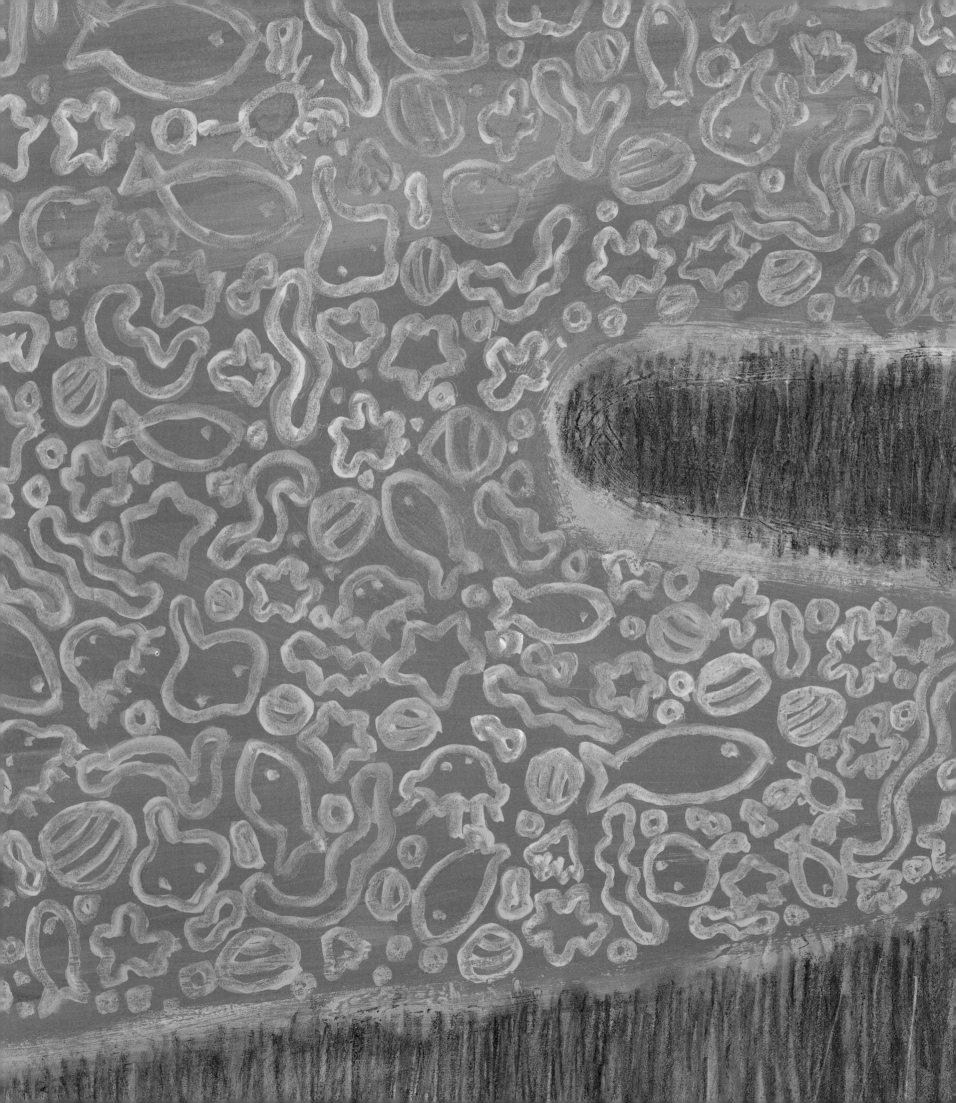

My fingers stretch out
Bays and inlets reach far into the land
Gulfs, seas, sounds and channels
　　lead to me
　　　　and into me
They are me

I am here day and night,
heaving,
    raging,
        lying still
scraping away at some land
    and putting it someplace else,
        bit by bit
My shape changes,
    as it has for ages
sometimes growing,
    sometimes shrinking
        never staying still

The sun
    so many millions of miles away
      heats my water,
which turns into clouds and storms
    that rain into me
      and it starts all over again

The moon
so far out in space
pulls at me
and then lets go
so my tides go in and out,
ebb and flood

First I was discovered
  (even though I was here first)
and then conquered
  by men in big ships
    who named me
I've been crossed and probed,
  charted,
    studied,
      dirtied

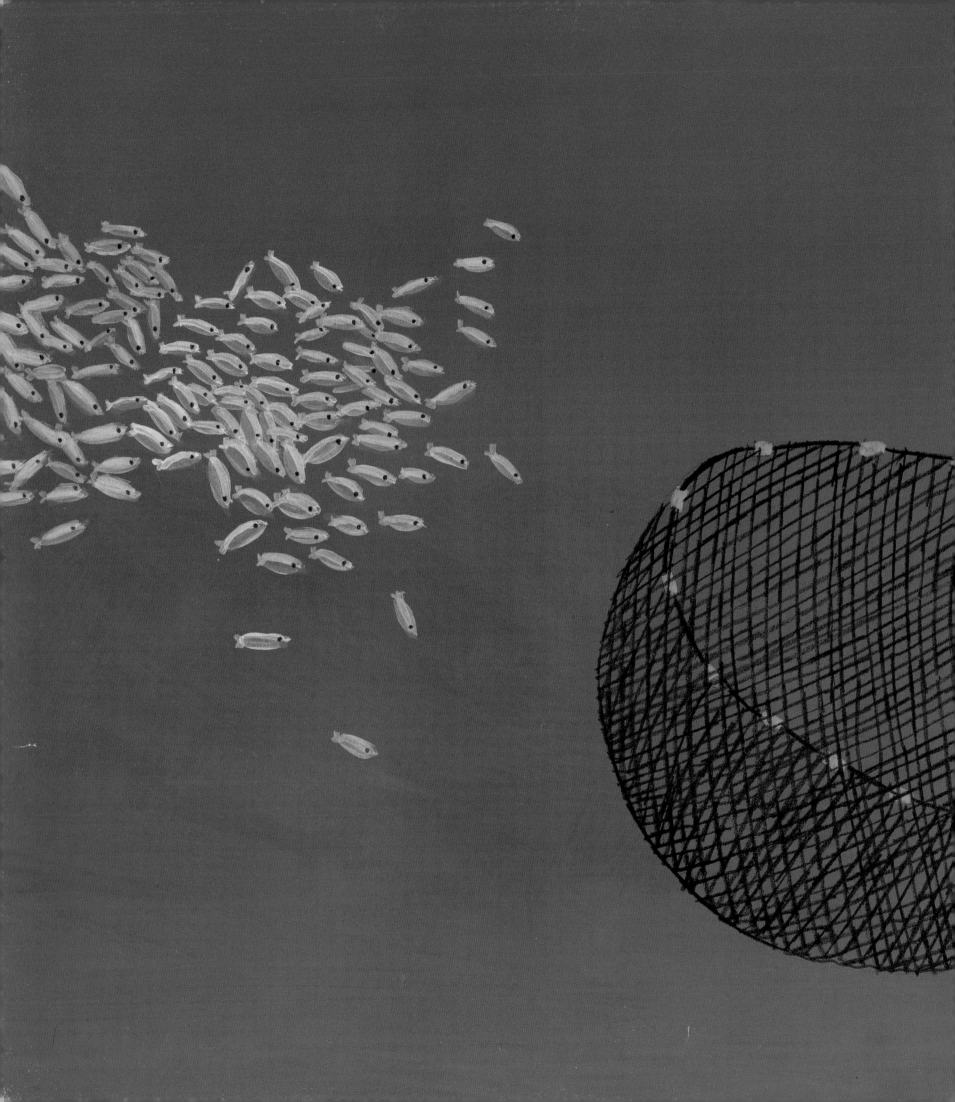

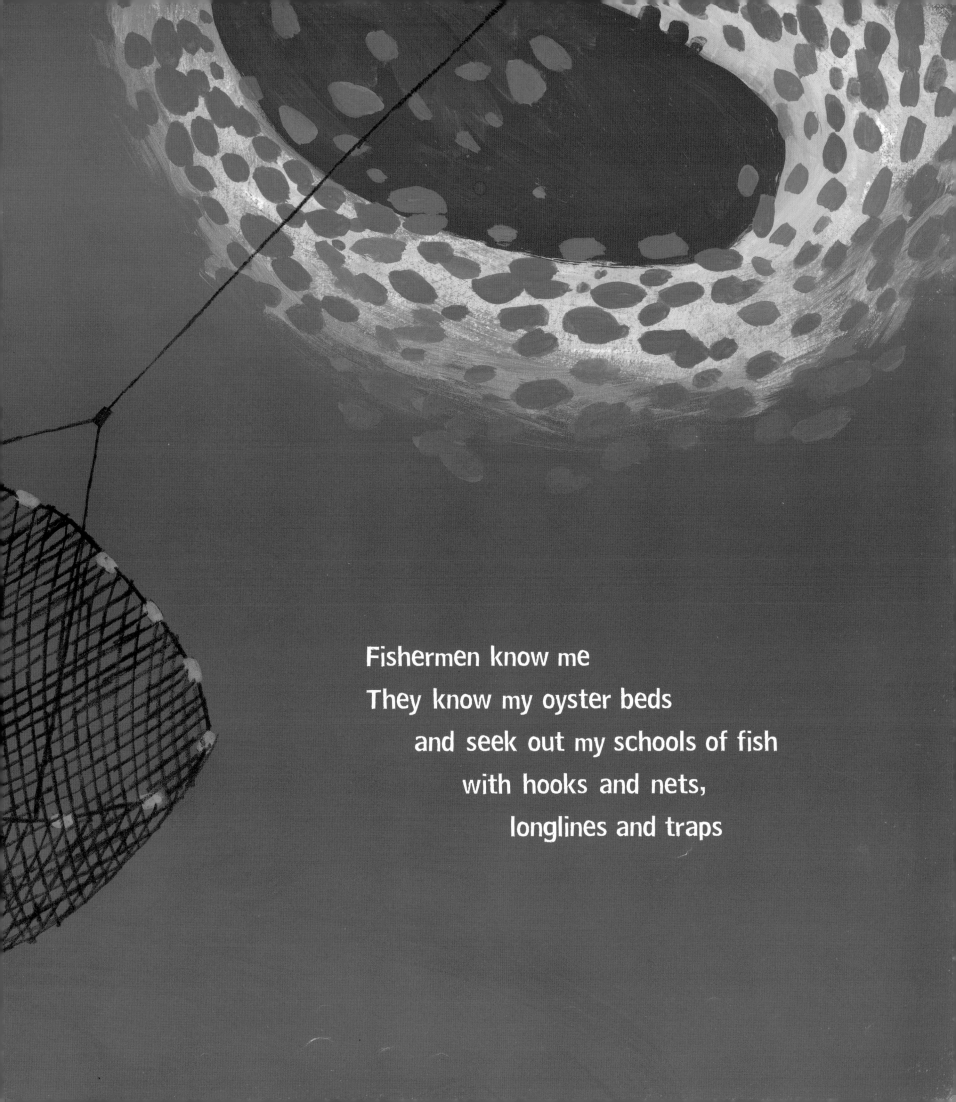

Fishermen know me
They know my oyster beds
    and seek out my schools of fish
    with hooks and nets,
        longlines and traps

Artists paint pictures of me
with cerulean,
cobalt and ultramarine

erable, both small and great beasts. *the Holy Bible* Oh sou

thur Rimbaud I have bathed in the poem Of the Sea... *Arthur Rim*

and majesty of the ships, And the magic of the sea. *Henry*

Ocean, who is the source of all. *Homer* All the rivers run

and of the sea, and the drops of rain, and the days of eterni

Lewis Carroll The sun was shining on the sea, Shining with all hi

n And the pleasant land. *Julia A. Fletcher Carney* The sea is calm

e night. *Walt Whitman* And alone d ever The kings of the s

And poets know me with their beautiful words

The dancing shadow of your airplane
skips over wave over wave

with dolphins who sing and race
with skates and whales and fish that fly

Seagulls sing to me
Sand and pebbles
   rattle and clatter a chorus
   as I rush in
      and pull away

My words crash and whisper in your ear

Don't forget I am here

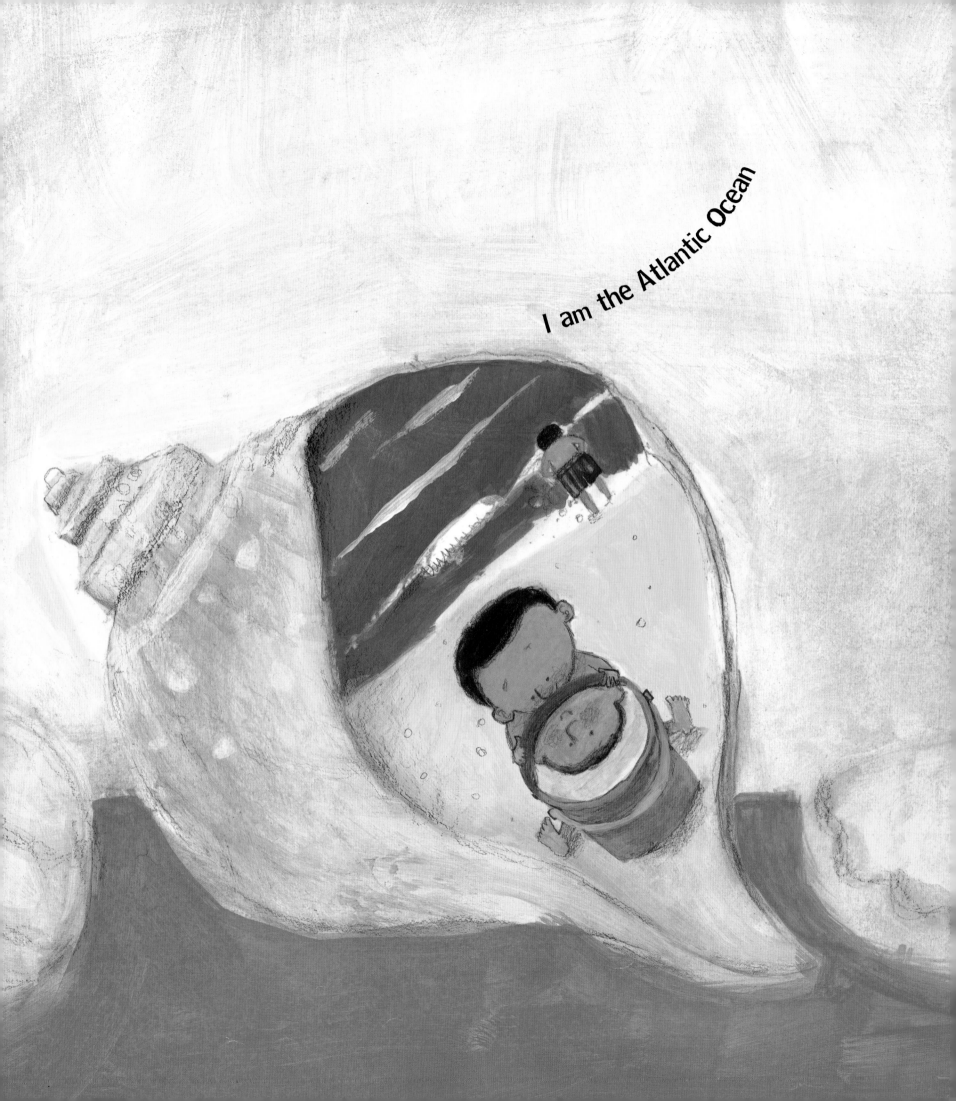

I am the Atlantic Ocean

Some Things About Me

I am not the earth's largest ocean, that's the Pacific. But I have many miles of shoreline because of my inlets, bays, gulfs, seas, sounds and channels. Some people think of all the earth's oceans as one, the World or Global Ocean.

If you were to empty me of all my water, you would find deep trenches (the Puerto Rico Trench is 8,648 meters deep—you could fit Mount Everest in the Puerto Rico Trench and only a little bit would stick up), wide basins and the earth's longest mountain range, the Mid-Atlantic Ridge.

I move about in giant currents, like the Gulf Stream and the Brazil and North Atlantic Currents, bringing warm weather to Ireland and dry winds to Africa.

I have been around for ages. Though I am from millions and millions of years of rain, I am the earth's youngest ocean. In the beginning the earth had one ocean, the Panthalassa.

I continue to grow, a couple of inches wider each year. What will I look like 200 million years from now, I don't know.

But for as old as I am, and as strong as I can be, I am in danger. What doesn't belong in my water are chemical and people wastes, oil and garbage. Please treat me with respect!